SPOOKED AT SMOKY STADIUM

PARANORMAL COZY MYSTERY

HAUNTED HISTORIES
BOOK THREE

LYNN M. STOUT

CHAPTER 1

"Well, this isn't bad at all," Ollie said as we pulled into the parking lot of the giant football stadium.

It was a sunny day, and the stadium shone brightly, giving off a welcoming, friendly vibe.

A cool breeze blew over us, hinting at even colder days to come. But for now, it was perfect. Gabby spread her wings and let the air flow through her grey feathers. She fluffed the feathers around her neck and made a low purring sound that confirmed she felt as content as I did.

"Let's see what's under it before we start feeling too confident," Tyler grumbled.

"Yeah, we've been fooled before," Leo added.

I listened to the banter between the team members and tried to ignore their prejudgements.

This was going to be difficult for me, there was no doubt about it. There were rumors that a serial killer's remains were under the stadium. I knew it was a long shot, but couldn't help wondering if he was the one who hurt Sophie. And as if that wasn't terrifying enough, it was also rumored that he was one of the spirits who was causing trouble. This investigation would be personal and dangerous.

We stood before Gate 21 wondering what we should do next when a man wearing sweatpants and a t-shirt with the team's logo emblazoned across it came jogging up to us.

"Jackie?" He called my name while looking at Emily. Of course, he was looking at Emily. She had grown into her new role in an astoundingly short amount of time, taking her new position as head of the research team for the crew very seriously. And, of course, she was the youngest and most adorable of us all. But I won't tell Tyler that.

"No, that's Jackie," Emily said, pointing at me. "I'm Emily, head researcher," she added with a proud smile.

Credit to him, his face only slightly registered disappointment as he turned to me and extended his hand.

"Jason Stewart," he said. "I'm the one who called you. We are trying to keep all of this quiet, you know, so the team doesn't get distracted and the students don't decide to start investigating on their own. You know how college kids are. Nice bird," he added.

"Thank you." I ran a hand down Gabby's back. "Her name is Gabby. So, what's been happening here, Jason?" I asked as he led us through the main gate. We walked down a long sloping ramp, and the air grew cool and damp. And it smelled strange, a combination of chemicals, cleaning products and rot.

"Well, you'll see as we get to where we're going. The actual entrance to what used to be classrooms and labs for the forensic anthropology department is just above us along the sidewalk. There are a series of hallways and classrooms under the stadium. We can also access it through the actual stadium itself though, which is what we're doing now since they closed off the other entrance. Again, trying to keep the students out of the area."

"Why are you so worried about the students?" Leo asked. "What do you think they are going to do?"

I could sense Leo was mildly offended, and I didn't blame him. He and Emily weren't much older than the very students Jason was insulting.

"Mostly it's for their safety. This is a very old

building. Things are not up to code and it hasn't been used in about a decade. And then now, with all that's happening with the ghos-, well, with whatever is happening, it's become even more dangerous."

"What got all this started?" Emily asked. "If these classrooms have been down here for so long, why are you just now worried about it? Especially if you aren't using them any longer."

We had finally reached the door to the wing of the building that used to house the department and paused while Jason explained.

"Well, the university had to start cleaning up. Like I said, the area is out-dated and not up to code. With football season coming up, and over one hundred thousand fans sitting directly on top of it, we have to make sure it's sound structurally. It is, but, you know, it's old. So we started renovating and cleaning out the area. As we dug into the job, some of the maintenance folks and the contractors began to see and hear strange things. Then it became even more pronounced."

Jason sighed. "Look, let's go on in. There's so much I can show you, and this will all make more sense."

I didn't tell him that what he was already

saying made perfect sense to us, especially based on what we had already experienced.

The vibe under the stadium was definitely different from the sunny outdoors. The narrow hallways were painted a sickly grey. The floors creaked under our feet as scarred and damaged wood cried out to be salvaged. We crowded into the hallway, bumping into each other.

Unfortunately, after the drive, nature was calling and that gave me a terrific opportunity to experience what they called a bathroom in this place. Jason directed me around a corner that led into what I thought was a closet. Certain he'd made a mistake in where he pointed for me to go, I carefully opened the door. Yes, it was a closet, but a closet that held a toilet that was, oh my gosh, up three steps? Why in the world was that the setup here?

"Ollie? I'm sending you Gabby, okay?" I called out. There wasn't room for the two of us.

"Yup," I heard in reply. Gabby didn't need to be told twice and immediately flew the short distance to land on Ollie's shoulder. She didn't want to be in the bathroom closet any more than I did. Luckily for Gabby, she could go anywhere.

Despite my discomfort of literally sitting on the throne, I did my business and returned to the group, who were deep in animated discussion.

"What's going on?" I asked as I approached them.

A small woman stepped out from behind everyone and smiled at me. She was so tiny she reminded me of the woman in Poltergeist who declared, "This house is clean." I wondered if she would say the same about this stadium.

She didn't.

Instead, she made it clear that nothing about where we stood was safe, much less clean of any evil.

"You shouldn't be here," she said ominously. "This place is dangerous."

Jason sighed and looked from the woman to me and back again. "This is Dr. Margo Wright," he said. "She teaches in the forensic anthropology department. When all the hoopla started up over here, she came to visit one day and let herself in. And, well, now she is here most days and…"

As Jason's words trailed off, Dr. Wright watched him with one eyebrow raised and her lips pursed. While obviously annoyed by his words, she appeared to enjoy the discomfort her presence created in him.

Shifting gears, she looked at me and smiled again.

"Jason is afraid to use the g-word," she said with air quotes. "Afraid if he calls it what it is, the boogey man will get him."

"Who is your boogey man?" I asked, halfway joking.

"Kaleb Smith," she said without hesitation. "A confirmed serial killer. He donated his body to the medical department and his brain to the Neural Deviance Project. Now his bones are here... somewhere."

"What's that project you mentioned?" Emily asked.

"Neural Deviance Project. It was a study about the neurological and psychological differences in the brains of serial killers compared to non-criminals. They looked at things like structural differences, chemical imbalances, things like that."

Emily nodded as Dr. Wright continued. "The body itself was donated to the Body Farm next door. His remains were moved again but seem to have been misplaced. Then, when this crew here," she jerked her thumb towards Jason, "decided to start mucking around with the resting place of not just Smith but also the other spirits down here, everything started going to hell, literally."

"Wait. What? Did you say Body Farm?" Tyler asked. "What is that?"

"Yes, I said Body Farm. It's next to the hospital, just across the river. Officially, it's called the Anthropology Research Facility. It's where we study the process of human decomposition in various scenarios."

"Like what?" Leo asked.

"We place bodies in different environments, like under a shady tree, versus out in the sun. Or in the trunk of a car, or in a shallow grave, and then document how the body reacts. It sounds horrible, but really, it's done with incredible respect and with donated bodies. Ultimately, it helps law enforcement solve crimes." Dr. Wright said.

"How?" Ethan asked, his pen poised at the ready.

"Well, one way is by helping establish the time of death. We study how bodies decompose in different environments, like I said. And added to that, it helps them understand different environ-mental effects, like temperature and even insects and other wild animals. Also, it's a training ground for investigators," she finished.

"Wow, I had no idea all that was going on. How

did you discover the journey of Kaleb Smith to here? How do you know it's actually him and that he donated his body to these programs?" Emily asked.

"He told me," Dr. Wright said.

"You were able to interview him before he died?" Emily asked.

Dr. Wright hesitated. "No...not exactly."

CHAPTER 2

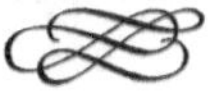

"Well, we can probably leave Clara and Ethan alone this time around," Ollie said as we unpacked and set up our belongings in the women's locker room.

"Why do you say that?"

"Because we have Dr. Wright. She seems to know everything. And she's actually talked to Kaleb Smith's spirit. First, it's nice that we don't have to convince her of anything, and second, she seems pretty knowledgeable. She could be really helpful."

I nodded. Ollie was correct, but I felt I would always need Clara. She was the only way I was going to continue to learn about my own burgeoning psychic abilities. And for that matter, could we trust that Dr. Wright really spoke to

Smith? Or was she just trying to insert herself into our investigation?

"What's going on, sis? You look like you're lost in another world."

Gabby squawked her agreement from the top of a set of lockers.

I hesitated, unsure if I was ready to put into words what I was feeling. Unsure if I even could put them into words.

"Everyone says this Smith guy was a serial killer. Well, no, let's backup. They don't just say it, we know it, right? It's been proven?"

Ollie nodded.

"He was a serial killer. We know this. However, we still don't know who killed Sophie. I'm afraid now that her case has gone cold, we never will. Am I trying to create something out of nothing here?"

"Connection," Gabby squawked.

I glanced up at her. She was looking at me with those piercing black eyes, her head slightly cocked to the side.

"Yes, I feel like there's a connection. Feeling being the key word here. It's a feeling."

"Like intuition?" Ollie asked. "Like a psychic intuition?"

"Ollie, I just don't know. I mean, yeah, sure. I get these feelings, these intuitions. They come and go. Clara says, I need to focus more on them and really learn how to embrace them. That way I can use my abilities whenever I want. But how do I practice when every time I'm supposed to use them, it's really important? Like now? There's nothing I want more than to know who did this to my sister. To get revenge on them for everything. But what if I go into this believing it was Kaleb Smith and I'm wrong?"

"Why do you have to make that decision right now? Why can't it just be another investigation and you trust yourself, your intuition, to know what to do when the time comes?"

That hadn't occurred to me, and I stopped in my tracks. From the moment I found Sophie's body, everything and everyone around me changed. I became less important. My thoughts, feelings, beliefs... simply stopped mattering. Instead, the only thing that mattered was the gap Sophie's death left in our lives.

If I found out who killed her, I could finally fill that gap. I snapped my fingers.

"If I'm wrong and it's not him, then I'm still right where I've always been and I can't name her killer. I can't even help at all. But if I'm right, and it is Kaleb Smith, then I can give the police something that they could work backwards from. Then they could confirm it, right? And then everything would be okay again."

Ollie looked at me with the same look Gabby was giving me. Both of them with their head sideways, their eyes boring into mine.

"What? Both of you. Knock it off."

"What is this case about, then? Is it about naming the killer? Is that your motivation here? In every other case, we try to solve the reason behind why the spirit is still around. We try to get to the reason for the haunting. We never really got the okay to focus on Sophie's story. Why is it different now?"

"Well, for one thing, I might end up face to face with the person who killed my sister," I snapped. "That's never been an option before. Should I just ignore it?"

"No, of course not. I just don't want you to pin so much on this being the one that you forget about everything else. I'm worried about you."

Something inside me snapped, and I knew I was finished with not only this conversation but also with the psychoanalysis.

"I'm just fine, thanks," I muttered. "Look, let's just focus on the job we have in front of us. I'll manage the other stuff myself, including my own therapy, okay?"

"Yeah, okay," Ollie said. I saw from the corner of my eye that she looked at Gabby. They both shook their heads.

I left Ollie and Gabby to shake their heads over my pathetic self, and went back to the main area of our investigation. Leo was already set up with his recording equipment and Ollie would set up her sound as soon as she was finished commiserating with Gabby over my lack of personal insight.

Dr. Wright was hanging around, waiting for Tyler. He said he wanted to get her on camera and ask a few more questions about the Body Farm and her role at the university. She would be a fountain of useful information, and I applauded his ambition.

When we first began doing the show, we were told with absolute certainty that we could not investigate my family's personal tragedy. But now, with Rachel Adams, our new and greatly improved producer on our side, I felt like it might be a possibility. And apparently everyone else did too. Emily and Tyler were already planning how to incorporate it into the filming, and Tyler even asked me to be on camera for an interview.

"That would be a hard no," I told him as Emily sidled up to me.

"Jackie! There you are," she said. "I've been looking for you. Listen, I've been doing some more research on the whole Kaleb Smith thing and I think I can put him in your town around the time of, uh, Sophie's, uh..."

I saved her and filled in the word "murder" to let her off the hook.

"Um, yeah. It's hard to say. Anyway, did the police ever look into him? Do you know?"

"No, I can't say for certain, but I don't remember his name coming up at all. Maybe he wasn't on their radar yet?"

"Yeah, that checks out. If I'm right and it was him, it's possible Sophie may have been one of his first victims. If not the actual first one."

She paused and gave me that same damn look Ollie and Gabby gave me. Head to the side, concern in her eyes.

"Are you okay?"

I needed to put a stop to this. I had half the team telling me not to focus on him being the killer so I wouldn't get hurt and the other half trying to prepare me just in case he was the killer, so I wouldn't get hurt.

Either way, I was going to get hurt. And I sure

would not spend the entire shoot as the 'sister of the victim' being handled with kid gloves. I had a job to do, and I was the boss, after all. I needed to be in charge, strong and the one who worried about the team, not the one the team was worried about. I wasn't some breakable doll.

"Yes, I'm fine. Let's get on with this, okay? No more talk of Sophie. I will handle that myself. My sister, my story, my issue. Okay? Can I please get everyone to focus on the haunting right here? This Smith character isn't the only one here, and we have a show to do."

I must have been louder than I realized. The entire room had frozen, and I scanned the shocked faces around me. Ollie was behind me with Gabby on her shoulder. Emily had moved away, and Tyler and Dr. Wright stopped their interview. Leo's camera hung at his side, his eyes downcast.

Great. Now I was the one letting my personal stuff interfere.

"I'm going for a walk. I'll be back shortly."

In a huff, I started through the maze to get back outside and immediately became hopelessly lost. I stopped and looked behind me, hoping someone was brave enough to follow and show me how to get out of the bowels of the stadium, but no one was there. I was officially scarier than a ghost.

CHAPTER 3

When I passed what appeared to be the same bulletin board for the third time, I admitted to myself that I was lost. I pulled my cellphone out intending to call for help but, of course, the old building was also a bomb shelter back in the day and there was no signal this far under.

I tried a few classroom doors hoping to get access to a window. That would help me envision where in the building I was and ideally, I could figure out from there how to get out or at least get back to the team.

Most of the doors were locked, but there were a few left ajar. I opened one and felt a freezing draft swoosh over me. Looking around, I rubbed the goosebumps down. Sure enough, a row of windows sat high on the concrete wall. They were dusty and grimy, and impossible to see out of. I looked around the old lab at the rusty stools and crumbling desks. Nothing to stand on. Nothing safe, at least.

In frustration, I flopped to the ground. Not as easy as it sounds. My knees and lower back cried out angrily as they were thrust into a position they were not used to.

Great, now my body was as damaged as my mental state. What was I going to do?

In the silence of the room, I whispered out loud to myself.

"I need to find Kaleb Smith and just ask him. According to Dr. Wright, he communicates. So that's it. Find his ghost and ask him. That's the simplest thing. But then why should I believe anything he says? What makes me think a killer is suddenly going to have morals and tell the truth? The police are no use. They dismissed several suspects ages ago and probably never even looked into Smith. But can I blame them? Why would they even think to question him? What was it Emily said? She thought she could place him in town at the time. If that's true, then maybe..."

I let my words fade away as I sat on the floor in heaven knows where while the team was going forward doing their jobs. So far on this shoot, I'd done nothing but moan and groan and be cranky. I definitely wasn't doing my job.

Was it possible to combine the two things? Could I possibly carry out the investigation and make the show that we came here to create while solving Sophie's murder at the same time? And who was I to think I could do both when professionals still hadn't solved it?

Totally disgusted with myself, I pushed my body to my knees and then, using a questionable stool, pulled myself to standing. I'd definitely tweaked my back, so that was fun.

Running my hands through my hair, I turned again to look around the room and stopped dead in my tracks. There stood three figures. I was sure they weren't there before, but they were there now and they were all looking at me.

"She's looking at us," one of them said.

"No, she's looking through us," another corrected him.

"No, past us. She can't see us, right?" The third waved his hand in front of his face.

"Of course she can't see us. We're ghosts, you idiot," the second one said.

"No, watch. She's changing where she's looking as each of us speaks. She can see us," the first ghost announced.

"Now who's the idiot?" The third ghost asked.

They grew silent, still looking directly at me. They were correct. I had been shifting my gaze as each one spoke. The fact they called me out on it was jarring. It was my turn to speak, or to do something.

"Uh, hi," I said, waving my hand briefly. "Yeah, I can see and hear you."

The three of them jumped and skittered backwards in fear.

"It's okay," I said. "I won't hurt you."

Why I said that, I don't know. It's not like I could hurt a ghost. What was I going to do? Turn on a high-powered fan and blow them to the next room? Although, to be fair, I had to wonder if what we did at the mansion was painful to Julia.

The first ghost must have thought the same as I did. He recovered quickly.

"Oh, it's okay guys, she won't hurt us. Phew, thank goodness," he snarked.

"Yeah, gosh, wow, that sure was close," the third one said as the second one passed his hand across his face and pretended to flick sweat from his brow.

I started to think I had the Three Stooges in front of me.

"Who are you?"

"Who are you?" They asked in unison.

"I'm Jackie Thompson. I'm doing a documentary on the hauntings down here. The hauntings which seem to be you."

That was met with silence as they looked uncomfortably from one to the other.

"We don't want to make you leave or anything. We just want to do whatever you want. However we can help you find peace."

My attempts to explain were met with uproarious laughter.

"Find peace, she says."

"Right, like that'll ever happen."

"Especially with you-know-who around."

When the last one spoke, the other two turned on him. One swatted his arm but only left tendrils of mist that joined them together briefly until they settled back into their own forms.

"Who is 'you-know-who'?" I asked, fully expecting they would name Kaleb Smith. I imagined that he controlled everything down here and was keeping all these souls locked away, miserable and desperate for -

"Dr. Wright," one of them blurted.

"Harry! Knock it off! We don't talk about her to anyone."

"I know her!" I said. "Dr. Wright is helping us. She even told us about Kaleb Smith." I lowered my voice. "Is he around here?"

"I don't know," the ghost named Harry said. "But I do know you shouldn't trust Dr. Wright."

"Yeah, she isn't your friend, and she's not helping you."

With that last statement, all three disappeared into thin air. I know I stood with my mouth hanging open because what else was I going to do? I needed to tell the rest of the team as soon as possible.

With the words that Dr. Wright was not our friend still ringing in my ears, I noticed a piece of paper flutter to the ground in front of the class-room door. I walked towards it and bent to pick it up, but it fluttered away from me, back in the direction I had come from. This continued all the way through the halls, around corners, up and down stairs, until finally, I could hear the team just ahead of me.

With a quick "thank you" to whoever, or whatever, had led me back, I jogged towards the group with an apology on my lips.

As always, they were kind, forgiving and understanding and I was appreciative.

"What's the plan, then?" Emily wisely lowered her voice. "Do you want me to do more research? Or just let it be?"

I glanced around quickly and motioned towards Dr. Wright with my eyes. Emily nodded, understanding my signals.

"Let's just get on with the investigation," I said. "We'll work the rest out when the time comes."

Everyone nodded along as I spoke, and Emily gave me a wink. Meanwhile, Dr. Wright was still hanging around on the edges of the group. We needed to get rid of her so we could talk openly. She seemed to hang on our every word.

I raised my voice. "Okay team, let's do an equipment check."

My brilliant team picked up the hint and after several minutes of checking and rechecking equipment and discussing mundane tasks, Dr. Wright finally sighed.

"I'm leaving," she said. "This is obviously the boring part of your job. I'll be back tomorrow when you're actually doing something."

We muttered our goodbyes, then as soon as she

was out of hearing, I pulled the team in close and told them every single thing that happened while I was lost.

Everyone was excited to meet the three ghosts and hoped for more information from them. We decided we would look for the room again tomorrow. We also agreed to keep all information private and not tell Dr. Wright anything we discovered, at least for now.

"Especially as it relates to Kaleb Smith being Sophie's killer," I added.

As everyone made their plans for the next day, Ollie pulled me aside.

"Hey, sis? I need to talk to you."

We huddled in a private corner and I faced her with my hands on my hips.

"What is it?" I asked. "I already said sorry for before. And you know I'm really sorry for how I talked to you and treated you...and Gabby," I added, glancing at my parrot, who still perched on Ollie's shoulder. I patted my shoulder, but Gabby didn't fly over to me.

"I, well, we," she glanced at Gabby, "are a little worried that you're still convinced this Kaleb Smith is guilty of killing Sophie, especially with no actual proof. I mean, obviously he was a bad guy and did terrible things, but there's no reason to believe that he did anything to Sophie. What will happen if you accuse him, but it turns out that he's innocent?"

I hesitated while forming my words, then spoke slowly as my thoughts tumbled out of me.

"Ollie, I need it to be him. It's time. I need to put this all behind me and move on without this around my neck. It just has to be."

"I completely get that. But I think it's important for you to stay impartial. Not come down hard on either side, you know? Because now, I have to ask the opposite question. What if it's not him? What if you could move on and put all this behind you without knowing who it was?"

That thought had never occurred to me. I didn't see how I could move on without knowing who did this. I'd always felt it was my job to find the answer and until I did, I was failing my entire family. If I had some sort of psychic ability, then didn't I need to use it? It was the only way to find peace within myself and to make things right again.

I shook my head.

"It just has to be him."

The camera opens with a wide aerial shot of Smoky Stadium, the bright autumn sun casting long shadows across the field. As the shot transitions to the main entrance, Tyler Reed steps into view, standing confidently at Gate 21, his signature polished look in full display. He adjusts his blazer, flashing a brief smile to the camera before beginning his introduction.

"Good evening, I'm Tyler Reed, and welcome to another captivating episode of 'Haunted Histories,' where we uncover the chilling truths hidden beneath familiar landmarks. Today, we investigate Smoky Stadium, a place known for roaring crowds and unforgettable games. But beneath the surface lies something far darker."

The camera pans to a view of the sprawling

stadium stands, gradually descending to the shadowy tunnels below. Tyler begins walking towards the entrance, his tone shifting to one of intrigue.

"Rumors swirl around this site, suggesting the restless spirit of serial killer Kaleb Smith haunts the very foundations of this stadium. His remains, misplaced during university renovations, are believed to be buried somewhere beneath these stands. But is his spirit truly responsible for the strange occurrences here? And could his connection to this place lead to uncovering even darker secrets?"

A cut to Jackie Thompson and the crew walking alongside university staff shows them entering the underground hallways, their flashlights flickering against the cold, grey walls.

"Joining me, as always, is Jackie Thompson and her dedicated team of paranormal investigators. With state-of-the-art equipment and an unrelenting drive to uncover the truth, they aim to determine if Kaleb Smith's spirit still lingers, and if his presence is linked to the escalating disturbances reported by staff and students."

A shift to Dr. Margo Wright standing confidently by the entrance, speaking to the crew.

"Dr. Margo Wright, a forensic anthropologist

familiar with the history of these halls, believes the disturbances began when renovations disturbed the resting place of Kaleb Smith and others who were laid to rest here. Her insights may lead us to the answers we seek."

"What lies beneath the surface of Smoky Stadium? Is it merely the echoes of history, or do the spirits of the past still walk these corridors? Tonight, we step into the unknown, seeking answers to questions that have haunted this site for years."

"Stay tuned as we uncover the mysteries lurking within Smoky Stadium. I'm Tyler Reed, and this is 'Haunted Histories.'"

The scene fades to black.

CHAPTER 5

"We're ready when you are," Emily said. She was looking at me in an odd way, as though not sure what my response would be.

"Okay, let's go then," I snapped.

It was a quiet group that trudged through the narrow hallways under the stadium. Normally we would have been a bit rowdy, fired up for the adventure and the challenge. But this time, it was different. And it was my fault.

I knew I had to get my head in the game and stop obsessing over the situation with Sophie, but it was hard when everyone else was obsessing too. Still, my focus was shifted in a dangerous direction and it would not help anyone or anything for me to be in this state. No matter what everyone else did or didn't do, this was my issue and mine alone.

"Does this feel right?" Tyler asked as we made what felt like yet another left turn. "We aren't going in circles, are we?"

"No, I'm pretty sure this is correct," I said. "Although last time I was lost so I could be a little turned around. Anything on the EVP?" I asked Emily.

"Oh, yes. Lots. Mostly just jumbles of static, though. Nothing clear."

The EVP captured unexplained words or sounds and would tell us if there was paranormal activity in the area. Hopefully, it would tell us when we got closer to the three ghosts I'd met earlier. I also hoped they would be more receptive to me and the team this time around.

Just as Emily exclaimed, "Oh, I got something!" We saw a figure ahead. It was standing in front of what used to be a snack machine. The machine was old and rusty and obviously empty of whatever snacks and sweets it once held. The figure was not one of the three ghosts I'd already met. This one wore a lab coat and wore a skinny black tie. He also wore old style glasses with thick black rims and carried a clipboard.

We slowed down and approached him slowly and carefully. He didn't seem to realize we were there and didn't turn around.

"Um, hello?" Tyler started.

The figure didn't move or react at all.

"Hello," Tyler tried again, a little louder. Still nothing. He looked at me and shrugged.

I shook my head, just as confused as he was. I didn't recall ever meeting a spirit form that couldn't or wouldn't respond to us. I wondered if he could even hear us.

"Maybe he's not able to speak?" Leo whispered.

"Or maybe he is just so used to not being seen he doesn't realize we're talking to him?" Emily guessed.

"Maybe...," I mused. I scooted through our small group and stood beside the figure. I looked directly at him and opened my mouth to speak. At that moment, he turned and walked directly through me.

I coughed and lost my breath for a moment. SStunned,I turned to the group for confirmation that what I thought had just happened really happened.

"What the-?"

"Are you okay?" Ollie asked. "That was the wildest thing I've seen yet!"

"Yeah, I'm fine," I gasped. I really was okay. Just a bit chilled and honestly, a little creeped out.

"He never even saw you," Emily said.

"Or if he did, it just didn't matter to him," Ollie added.

"Let's follow him." Tyler was already starting down the hallway after our mystery man and the rest of us quickly packed up and followed him.

It didn't take long before he turned into the very room where I'd met the other three ghosts. Was this some sort of clubhouse or meeting room for the spirits under Smoky Stadium?

Without hesitation we all trouped in after him with Tyler leading the way.

Sure enough, there were the three I'd met before. They were milling around talking and interacting with each other, but even they weren't interacting with our mystery man.

I gave the group a few beats to orient themselves. You never really get used to seeing ghosts and spirits, even in our job, and it often takes a few seconds at least to get your bearings and really comprehend what you are looking at.

While they were settling in and setting up recording devices, Harry looked over and said, "Oh! You're back!"

Without missing a beat, he introduced the rest of the ghosts to us.

"This is Martin, and this is Terrance. I'm Harry," he said. "And that guy over there is Dr. McAlister. And who are you?" He asked, looking from one team member to the other.

I introduced my group to the ghostly group, then immediately asked questions. I was afraid they would leave as abruptly as they had before and I wouldn't find out anything.

"Why did you leave last time I was here?" I asked. "And by the way, thanks for the help getting back to my group. I assume that was you leading me with the paper?"

"Yeah, you're welcome," Harry said.

"We left because we were finished talking, right guys?" Martin said.

"Well, I wasn't finished. I have so many questions," I glanced at Leo, who winked at me. He was recording, and I could see Ollie standing behind the ghosts with her sound equipment running. Hopefully, we would have some great footage here.

"It won't work," Terrance said, gesturing towards Leo and Ollie.

"What won't work?" Tyler asked. He was moving into interview mode and standing beside them.

"What you're trying to do. You won't get us on film."

"Yeah, and you won't get our voices either. No one ever has. Even Doc over there wasn't able to do it."

"What's his story?" Tyler asked, ignoring the warnings. "It's like he can't see us or even hear us."

"That's because he can't," Harry said. "He's different from us. Always has been."

"Do you know what happened to him?" Emily asked.

"Well, yeah, he died," Harry helpfully replied.

I swallowed my irritation and asked if they knew how he'd died.

They did not.

I wanted so badly to ask again about Kaleb Smith and find out if they really knew nothing or if they were just playing games earlier, but Tyler was in full interview mode. Despite the suggestion that we could not record them at all, Tyler was asking questions as Leo moved around them, setting up a good shot. Ollie stood her ground just behind, with the recording devices going full speed.

Emily and I stood to the side and watched and listened.

"Have you heard from Rachel?" She whispered.

Rachel was our producer and while she'd spent

a lot of time with us on the last location, Hawthorne Hall, she wasn't as hands-on this time around. She was helpful at times, but also a bit of a bother. She'd gotten under Leo's skin pretty quickly and didn't win anyone over when she started a fire to drum up attention and drama for the show.

"Not yet," I said.

We grew quiet as Tyler's questions got more serious. After discovering that the three arrived around the same time, in 1952, as fully articulated skeletons for use in the classrooms, they told us about some other visitors to the department.

"Lots have come and gone," Harry said.

"Yeah, some good and some bad. Usually, when they take the bodies out, the spirits go with them. If there's a spirit at all."

"Sure, we've seen plenty of bodies without the spirit attached. In fact, I'd say that's way more common, wouldn't you?"

The other two agreed.

"But when they took our bones out, we stayed," Terrance added, fanning his hands to his side. "Don't know why, though."

"Is anyone else here?" Tyler asked.

"Oh sure. A few other guys like Doc there. And a few women who mostly keep to themselves. A couple of fellas who hang out upstairs. They are the football crew, jocks mostly. They watch the games and if they can, they cause all sorts of trouble for the teams."

"Trouble like what?" Tyler asked. "And I don't know the game very well so ...,"

"You don't gotta know the game to see what they do. The best one is when a guy is running with the ball and it looks like he just trips and falls down? That's one of the jocks upstairs. Or when they throw the ball and it looks like it just goes sideways all of a sudden, that's them too. They are annoying, but pretty funny. And it breaks up the monotony around here."

I knew what Tyler was getting at when he asked again. "So anyone who scares you? Or is evil or trouble?"

"Not anyone who's a ghost like us," Martin said. "Like we told your friend there," he nodded at me. "Dr. Wright will act like your friend and get you to trust her, but believe you me, she ain't your friend. Watch your backs."

Once again, with those words, the other two reacted as though he shouldn't have said anything, and within seconds, the three disappeared again.

"Well, I hoped we'd get answers from the ghosts, but it looks like we're better off talking to the living," Tyler grumbled.

We were making our way back to camp and trying to make sense of what we'd learned so far.

No one mentioned Smith or any malevolent being beyond the pranks and silliness of the jocks upstairs.

But once again, we received a cryptic message about the treacherous Dr. Wright.

"Emily?" I said.

Before I could finish my sentence, she replied, "Already on it. I'll have some background on her, the ghosts, and Dr. McAlister within an hour."

I smiled my thanks.

"And thank you, Tyler. I could tell you were trying to get the information we need about Smith."

"No problem-o," he said, turning his head back towards me and tripping over an old chair that sat in the hallway.

It was time for me to make amends and let the team know where we stood.

I cleared my throat and everyone stopped to look at me.

"No, keep walking," I said. "It's easier if I don't have to look at each of you. I just wanted to apologize for being so cranky since we've been here." When I said cranky, Ollie coughed. "I know it's more than just cranky. I lost my focus and got all caught up with my sister's situation. The thing is, her murder is unsolved. And when I heard about a serial killer here, and there are a few connections to our hometown, I got a really strong feeling that I would find the killer here. That it would be this Kaleb Smith person and I could find justice for Sophie. And…no, that's not entirely true. It's more than that. I want to find justice for myself too. Everything changed when she died and it really affected me. I want things to be back the way they were."

Ollie took my hand and squeezed. "You know that's not possible, though, right? Things will never be the same. Time has passed, you're a different person now. We all are."

"Yeah, I know, but can't I at least try?"

The only sounds in the hallway were shuffling feet and heavy breaths, as no one seemed eager to reply to my question. No one except Gabby, that is.

She began flapping her left wing into my face repeatedly so I couldn't see well through her feathers.

"Knock it off, Gabby," I said.

She immediately did it again.

"Gabby!"

It didn't matter. She continued to irritate me with her flapping wing until I got the hint.

"Fine, I'm a different person and things have changed, okay? Happy now?" I said under my breath.

Gabby squawked her pleasure and stopped beating my face with her wing.

CHAPTER 6

Normally at this point in the investigation, Tyler and Emily have reached out to others involved in the situation and we are developing interviews and getting footage of the locals. However, this time, it was three ghosts that we tried to get information from and that failed miserably.

"I've found something," Emily said. "Our three friends are completely innocent. They donated their bodies to science and, through the process, they all ended up in the forensic science department under the stadium. They came from different places, but all died around the same time and from innocent causes. Harry was in a car accident. Martin and Terrance had heart attacks. Regarding Dr. McAlister, he was a professor here and disappeared in the early forties. No known cause of death or anything.”

“Wow,” Tyler said. “That’s really sad.”

“Yeah, I know.” Emily agreed.

“Okay, well, I have some information about Dr. Wright,” Tyler said once we settled back at our base. “Probably not as much as you’ve found though,” he nodded at Emily.

“Nope, go ahead,” she said. “I’m still researching her, so tell us what you’ve found. I’ll add anything else I know as we go.”

I took a moment to just appreciate how well my team worked together. With a satisfied smile, I sat back and listened.

“She has worked here for only a few years, it seems. And she took an immediate interest in all things haunted regarding the university. In fact, she actively sought paranormal activity when she arrived on campus and I suspect, despite what she says, that she already knew about the activity under the stadium.”

“So you think she came here on purpose?” Emily asked as she made a note on her iPad.

“Yes, I do.”

We all grew quiet as we thought about his words. Obviously, our three ghostly friends were intimidated by her and didn’t want to talk about her. And yet they completely blew off any discussion of Kaleb Smith being under the stadium.

"Emily, tell me again how we know Smith is here for sure?"

Emily scrolled back through her notes.

"Okay, I have access to the records for this department dating way back to the twenties. And I found our three ghosts' records already. They are easy to trace and what they told us is accurate, by the way. So, for Kaleb Smith..,"

Emily opened a tab on her laptop and turned it around for us to see. As she read from her iPad, she scrolled through her laptop.

"I've sent this file to each of you if you want to use your own devices to follow along."

Ollie sat beside me and looked over my shoulder as I opened my laptop. Tyler's laptop was already up and running. I don't know how he did it, young eyes for sure, but Leo followed along on his phone.

We scrolled through newspaper headlines and coroner reports and a few police reports. As Emily talked, we scanned the information she'd sent us and asked follow-up questions.

"They were onto him as early as nineteen seventy-four when he was suspected of killing three people throughout two states. With the way technology was back then, it was a fluke that they could even connect the three crimes. It only happened because two investigators in those two offices knew each other and communicated."

"Wow, what are the odds?" Tyler muttered.

"Not good at all. Really, it was a miracle. But unfortunately they weren't able to piece it together quick enough and Smith went on to kill another two people before they finally caught him. He was tried and convicted. He had a girlfriend on the outside who would visit him, but no one else. No one in his family and apparently no friends at all. Even his attorney gave up eventually, as he was difficult to talk to and always angry."

"What's this?" I asked, pointing to a hand-written letter that was scanned into a file.

"Ah, that's interesting," Emily smiled. "It's a letter written by one of his cellmates, when he could still have a cellmate, about the dangerous things he said. The gist of it is, he is evil, he will get revenge, and he will be back to do harm to those who harmed him."

"Lovely," Ollie added. "A real charmer, this one."

I noticed Leo swallow hard and nudged Ollie. We would need to be sure to check on him later.

Although considering what Emily did next,

maybe we didn't need to be worried. Without saying anything or drawing attention to herself, Emily stood and moved beside Leo. She sat close to him so their thighs touched. Then she continued.

"Kaleb Smith was attacked in the prison and almost died. It seems some of the other prisoners were tired of him calling himself a god of evil and other crazy stuff. Plus, he was always threatening them. After that, he was moved to solitary. Then, just a few months later, they found him dead in his cell. They do not know what happened."

"No idea? There had to be something. Suicide? Or someone got to him?" I asked.

"Right, you would think so. But he was lying on his bunk, eyes closed, nothing was awry in the cell and the cameras showed nothing unusual. Of course, he was on suicide watch and was searched all the time for anything he could use to harm himself, but nada," she shrugged.

"Now, this was during the time when a lot of research was beginning on personalities and brains and there was a lot of interest in what type of anomaly might exist in the physical brain of someone like him...not to mention the personality and other issues that create this type of person. His body went to a university in the northeast, where it was dissected and studied. Then he was packed up and sent to the Body Farm here. He had donated his body to science incidentally and requested that he ultimately be placed at the Body Farm."

"Strange request from someone who didn't seem to care about others," Leo muttered.

"Definitely," Emily agreed.

"Okay guys, we know Dr. Wright is very interested in him and even says he told her who he is so we have to talk to her as soon as possible and get some straight answers. Tyler, what else did you find out?"

"She didn't tell me any of what Emily said. In fact, she said much the opposite. She said she believes he was innocent and didn't commit any of those crimes. She got interested in his case when she was studying innocent people behind bars. His name came up a few times in her research and when she heard about what was happening here, she wondered if his spirit was restless and still here. And yes, she says that she talked to him. She also says he's angry, that part is true for sure, but it's not because he wants revenge or because he thinks he's a god of evil, it's because he was unfairly imprisoned."

"I think I would like to talk to her again and compare stories. Let's see why she believes what she says instead of the many, many reports we have here. What do you think?"

Before anyone could answer, Gabby squawked, "Danger Will Robinson, Danger!"

We all turned our heads to see none other than Dr. Wright standing in the doorway, hidden in the shadows. No one had heard her approach.

"I don't appreciate being called a liar," she said to Tyler. "When we talked, I told you the truth. How dare you question me like this? And behind my back? I thought we were friends."

Tyler stood and immediately tripped over his own two feet as he quickly crossed the space to stand before her.

"That's not what I meant," he stammered. "But you do understand there are two versions here. And we want to get to the bottom of it all."

"Right," Ollie said. "If Kaleb Smith is truly innocent and his spirit is still trapped here, maybe we can help him find peace."

I watched Dr. Wright's face closely, and when Ollie said those words; she blanched. It was as though she didn't want that to happen to him. I couldn't blame her. Helping him find peace was definitely not on my radar, either. In fact, I wanted the exact opposite for the killer of my sister.

"Or we can make sure he gets what he deserves, even in death," I muttered. Realizing I had said that very unprofessional comment out loud, I quickly tried to cover my tracks.

"I know he served his time and all, but..."

"We were hoping you could tell us what you know about Kaleb Smith. And how to contact him. How did you find him?" Tyler attempted to cover for me.

Dr. Wright's eyes darted around the room and she paused longer than needed to answer the question. It made me wonder briefly if she was about to lie to us.

"I know what you mean," she began speaking slowly. "This is difficult. So many alternative stories are out there. And yes, as you mentioned, I have heard it directly from him and I believe I know the real Kaleb Smith. Much better than those who claim to know him or claim to know what he did. Once you talk to someone first hand, it really can change your perspective. For instance, you've talked to Harry, Martin and Terrance, right? What do you think of those three?"

"They sort of remind me of the Three Stooges," Tyler said.

"Right," Emily added. "They give you the impression that they know a lot about what's going on around here, but they never really help quite like you think they will."

"They know more than they are saying," I added while mentally noting how she changed the subject and avoided the question of how she met Kaleb Smith.

Dr. Wright smile wryly and nodded. "Yes, that is what I've gotten from them as well. A lot of talk but not a lot of information."

"And what about Kaleb Smith?" Ollie asked. "A lot of talk or a lot of information? Or both?"

A loud crash from the hallway prevented her from answering as we all rushed to see what happened. Stumbling and fumbling over each other in our usual way of going through doors, we finally stood in the hall, scanning both directions for any indication of what caused the noise.

Of course, nothing was there. And that included Dr. Wright.

"What was that?" Emily asked.

"And where did Dr. Wright go?" Leo added.

I couldn't help but notice how close together they were standing and that their pinkie fingers kept touching. Something was definitely brewing between those two but that particular investigation would have to wait. Right now, we had a disappearing professor who knew more than she was saying.

We gathered in our makeshift headquarters and sat in a circle. Gabby preened atop a bookcase, occasionally squawking her commentary as if she were the team's supervisor. Her sarcastic interjections mirrored my own mood.

"Okay, here's what we know," I began, pacing as I talked. "The three ghosts, Harry, Martin, and Terrance, are obviously afraid of Dr. Wright. I think as long as we are talking to her, they are going to be suspicious of us. While they have told us some things, they still don't trust us enough to share everything. And we still know nothing about the actual reason we came, the unexplained interference with the games."

"Right, if we've got ghosts out there manipulating reality in real time, that would be groundbreaking, right?" Tyler added.

"Absolutely. So let's find out what's really going on. Tyler, can you pull game footage from the past few seasons?"

"Yeah, but what am I looking for?"

"I'll help," Ollie said with a smile.

"Great. And what do you think about sound recordings in the locker rooms, hallways, entrance to the field...anywhere else?" I asked.

"We can absolutely try, but our three friends were right. We didn't get a bit of recording or footage from talking to them before. Still, I see what you're saying. Any place where a team would need to be while preparing for a game is a good place to at least try." Ollie made a note. "If anyone thinks of anything else, let me know."

The team nodded, their faces serious and focused.

"And Leo," I said, "let's get close-ups on anything moving on or around the field. Even if it's just a flutter of dust."

Leo gave me a thumbs-up and started fiddling with his equipment. Gabby squawked approval from her perch.

With the plan in place, we split up to set everything in motion. I stayed behind, using the quiet time to think about what lay ahead. As much as I wanted answers about the stadium, I couldn't ignore the gnawing question about Sophie. My sister's murder had cast a shadow over my life, and if Kaleb Smith truly was innocent, I'd be back to square one. No justice, no closure.

"Connection," Gabby whispered, breaking my thoughts as she landed on my shoulder. I ran my hand down her back. She tilted her head, her beady eyes drilling into me as if she could read my mind.

"Yeah, I know," I muttered. "I just don't know what the connection is yet."

Gabby let out a low whistle and fluffed her feathers. "You will."

CHAPTER 7

That evening, we began the investigation in the stands overlooking the field. The stadium, quiet now, would roar with close to one hundred thousand fans on game day. But tonight, it was ours alone. The air was heavy, thick with anticipation. I held my breath as Tyler played back a clip from a previous game.

"We found this," he said, pointing at the screen.

I watched as a wide receiver sprinted down-field. His long legs moved effortlessly. Not a single defender was in sight. Then, just as he reached the goal line, he fell to the ground, and the ball tumbled out of bounds.

"So, Ollie said there was no reason for him to trip. And even if he just stumbled, he could have held onto the ball," Tyler said.

"Right, it's as if someone stuck out a foot and then stripped the ball," I said.

"Or someone pulled him," Emily added, squinting at the screen. "Look at the trajectory of his fall. It's not natural. If his arm was yanked, that explains the stumble and losing the ball."

I nodded. "Must be our other ghosts, our jocks. They've figured out how to manipulate objects and people. Alright, let's see if we can get something tonight. Good luck everyone."

We spread out, each taking a section of the stadium. Tyler and Emily surveyed the field. Ollie and Leo stayed in the press box with cameras and other equipment set up around them as they monitored their cameras and microphones.

Gabby and I stayed with them, watching the entire field and helping where we could.

As the hours ticked by, the first sign of activity finally showed up on one of Leo's cameras. His whispered voice crackled through my headset.

"Tyler, Emily, we've got movement down there. It's faint, but it's in the hallway, heading toward the field."

"Stay with it," I whispered. "I'm going down."

I made my way to the lower level, my flashlight casting long shadows on the concrete walls. As I approached the hallway, I saw Tyler and Emily coming towards me. As we reached the entrance to the field, the air shimmered like heatwaves on a summer road.

"Can you get that?" Emily's voice whispered through the headsets.

"Yeah, I can," Leo's voice came back. "It's like a distortion. Wait! There's something else out there. Can you guys see anything?"

We all turned our eyes to the field. I squinted but still saw nothing. Emily was already seeing it, though.

"Yeah, uh, three figures. Running up and down the field." I looked at her and shook my head as she held my arm and pointed.

Sure enough, after a few more seconds, their forms were solid enough and we could all see them.

Ollie's voice crackled over the headphones next. "Guys, I can hear them clearly. They are laughing and teasing each other."

"Want to try talking to them?" Emily asked me.

I hesitated. They seemed so immersed in their ghostly game, I wasn't sure how they'd react to an interruption. But we couldn't let the opportunity pass.

I nodded.

We stepped onto the field, and the jocks noticed us immediately. They stopped their game and ran towards us at a slow jog. When they were close enough, I called out.

"Who are you?"

One of them stepped forward, a tall figure with a cocky grin. "We're the team," he said. "And you're interrupting practice."

"Oh, sorry! What are you practicing for?" I tried to keep my tone light.

"For the game, of course," another ghost said, spinning a phantom football on his finger.

"Do you play the game, or do you cause problems for the actual players?" Emily's bold question hung in the air.

After a slight pause, the first one answered. "Look, it's boring down here. We're surrounded by science-types who are always studying. Football season is our time."

"So you know Harry, Martin, and Terrance?" I asked. "We know them too."

The ghosts grew quiet at the mention of the others. Their playful demeanor shifted, replaced by something darker.

"Yeah, we know them," the leader said finally. "But they don't mess with the game like we do.

They stick to their little corners, watching and waiting."

"Waiting for what?" Emily pressed.

"For the one," the ghost said. "The one who keeps us all here."

"Kaleb Smith?" I asked, taking a chance.

The ghost's grin widened. "Nah, not him. Her."

"Her?" all three of us echoed.

The second jock ghost nodded. "Sure, Dr. Wright. She's got big plans, you know. Plans that could take us all out of here for good."

"What does that mean? How would she do that?" I asked.

The ghost tilted his head, considering the question. "Not sure, exactly," he said finally. "But if she gets her way, it'll be big and bad and no one will have a choice."

"Let's hit the showers, boys," one ghost called out, and the entire group dissolved into the night. We were alone on the field.

"Everyone, let's meet inside," I said. "I want to see what we got and we really need to talk."

The team was unsettled, but also excited. If any of that transferred to video or recording, we would have a terrific show. Still, I could tell everyone's mind was racing.

To help us all focus, I began. "Dr. Wright is

obviously the key. If we are to believe all the ghosts here, she is up to something."

"And possibly working with Kaleb Smith," Ollie added. "What does she want to do? Help him escape? Cause harm to the other ghosts?"

"Whatever it is, it's not good," Tyler said. "We need to confront her."

Gabby squawked. "Danger Will Robinson!"

Her timing, as always, was impeccable.

The locker room felt colder than usual as Dr. Wright stepped inside, her eyes scanned the group like a hawk searching for prey. Her presence alone could shift the air, and for reasons I couldn't quite put my finger on, I felt my pulse quicken.

"You're back," I said in my best Captain Obvious voice.

"Jackie," she sighed. "It's time we talk. Privately."

Everyone froze. Then Tyler gave me a concerned glance, while Emily shifted closer, as if ready to intervene. Gabby, ever the watchdog—or watch-parrot—let out a soft whistle of disapproval.

I nodded. Then stood and shrugged. I tried to give the team an encouraging smile to let them know all was okay, but I don't think I succeeded.

She led me to a quiet corner, and we leaned on the wall facing each other.

"I thought you'd gone for the night," I said. "You disappeared on us after that loud noise."

"Obviously, I came back. I know you've been looking for answers," she folded her arms. "And I think it's time we have a proper conversation."

"Okay. I would like that. We have a lot of questions for you. The first one being, why does it appear you are manipulating us? Telling partial truths and not answering direct questions?"

Her lips curled into a tight smile. "Sometimes manipulation is necessary to uncover the truth. But if you can adjust your attitude and put aside your suspicions, I might be able to give you what you're looking for."

I ignored the 'adjust your attitude' comment and crossed my arms over my chest. "And what do you think I'm looking for?"

"Closure," she said simply. "About your sister. About Kaleb Smith."

I froze, my breath catching in my throat. I scanned our time at the stadium quickly, trying to remember if anyone had said anything about Sophie to her or accidentally in front of her. We'd talked openly about Smith's crimes, but not in relation to my sister.

"How do you know about Sophie?" I whispered, my voice trembling despite my best effort to remain composed.

Wright tilted her head, her eyes softening. "It's obvious, Jackie. The way you tense up whenever his name comes up. I know pain when I see it."

"He's a bad guy. Of course, one would react to his crimes. But yet again, you're deflecting. How do you know about Sophie?"

Wright leaned in, her voice dropping to a conspiratorial whisper.

"I can help you," she said. "But only if you trust me."

"I'm not sure you've given me much reason to," I countered. "We're done here."

As I turned my back, she said, "If you want the truth, we'll need to confront him together."

"Why?" I asked, still standing with my back to her.

"Because we want the same thing," she replied, her tone sincere. "Answers. When you get your answers, I will get mine."

Her words settled over me like a heavy blanket, and despite every instinct screaming at me to walk away, I nodded. "All right," I said against my better judgment.

The plan was simple, or at least as simple as it

could be when dealing with a ghost rumored to be a serial killer. Wright claimed she could summon Kaleb directly, but she needed me there to draw him out.

"Meet me in one hour," she said.

TYLER REED: TAKE 2

The camera opens with a low shot of the shadowy stadium corridors, the air thick with dampness and echoes of footsteps from decades past. Tyler Reed steps into frame, adjusting his microphone, his expression solemn.

"Welcome back to *Haunted Histories*. I'm Tyler Reed, and tonight, our journey beneath Smoky Stadium continues—into a labyrinth of forgotten classrooms, eerie hallways, and restless spirits. As we delve deeper, the line between the living and the dead becomes increasingly blurred, with secrets long buried threatening to surface."

The shot transitions to the team—Jackie, Ollie, Emily, and Leo—moving carefully through the dimly lit tunnels.

"Our investigation leads us to unsettling encounters with the spirits of this place—skeletal remains of the past, preserved under the guise of science, now bound to these halls by forces we don't yet understand. But among the spirits, not all are eager to share their stories."

The camera zooms in as the group freezes.

"Spectral apparitions walk these halls, occasionally caught on camera."

The camera catches what appears to be interference.

"As we attempt to gather answers, warnings continue to mount. Those we've spoken to remain wary, and hinting at hidden dangers and urging caution. Are all to be trusted?"

"As the mysteries deepen, so does the danger. Our team must navigate not only the world of the dead but the ambitions of the living. Can we trust Dr. Wright's intentions, or are we walking directly into the heart of something far more sinister?"

The scene fades on a shot of Jackie, standing alone on the field, her eyes scanning the darkened rows of empty seats. Gabby squawks in the distance, echoing eerily through the tunnels.

"One thing is certain—beneath the roar of game day lies a truth begging to be uncovered.

Stay with us, as we edge closer to unraveling the secrets hidden beneath Smoky Stadium."

The screen fades to black.

CHAPTER 9

"Why do you have to be there, sis?" Ollie asked for the third time.

"I suspect because he killed Sophie, and something about that connection will draw him out." I explained for the third time.

"I don't like it at all," she added.

Gabby flapped her wings and muttered, "no, no, no," over and over.

"I'll go with you," Tyler said.

I shook my head. "She was pretty clear that it had to be just me. Well, Gabby and me," I added.

"We've got you wired up," Emily said. "We can hear everything you say, and you will be able to hear us as well. We'll monitor from here, I guess."

I tapped my shoulder and Gabby flew to me. As we made our way through the stadium's lower level, following Dr. Wright's directions, Emily's voice crackled through my earpiece.

"You don't have to do this," she said. "We can find another way."

"Thanks, but this is the only way," I replied, my voice steadier than I felt. "If I don't face him, I'll never get the answers I need. And remember what all the other ghosts have said. Dr. Wright is involved too. I need answers from her as well."

As I rounded a corner, I saw a light flickering at the end of the hallway. I whispered to the team, "I'm here," then we all went silent.

Wright sat before a small candle. She was already murmuring words I didn't understand, her voice low and melodic. When she saw me, she smiled and motioned me closer.

"Sit," she said. "And be quiet. He'll be here soon." Then she went back to her strange words, ending with a command. "Kaleb, come forward. We mean no harm."

For a moment, nothing happened. Then, slowly, a figure materialized and within seconds, Kaleb Smith stood before us, his presence as chilling as the rumors had promised. I felt a wave of nausea rise in my stomach.

He cast a quick glance at Wright, then locked his eyes onto mine. "I know why you're here."

"Good," I said, keeping my voice firm and the bile down. "Then you know I want the truth."

He smirked, a cruel twist of his lips. "The truth? About what?"

"Kaleb...," Dr. Wright warned.

Smith stepped closer, his translucent form casting a shadow that shouldn't have been possible. "Fine. I didn't kill your sister," he said.

My heart stopped. I opened my mouth to argue, to call him a liar, but the certainty in his voice was unshakable.

"I see you are struggling to believe me," he said.

"If it wasn't you, then who was it?" I demanded.

"That's the question, isn't it?" he said, his smirk widening. "Not only was it not me, but her killer is still alive and closer than you know."

His words hit me like a blow, and I staggered back, the weight of them too much to bear. Wright reached out to steady me, her expression unreadable.

"I don't believe you," I said, my voice barely a whisper.

"I have nothing to gain by lying," he replied with a shrug. "But if you keep digging, you might not like what you find."

Before I could press further, Kaleb faded, his

form dissolving into the mist. I turned to Wright, desperate for answers, but her expression was guarded.

"He's telling the truth," she said. "I know he is."

"How?" I demanded. "How can you be so sure?"

Wright hesitated, then said, "Because I know who killed Sophie."

With those words, she turned and walked away. I tried to follow her, but Ollie suddenly appeared and held my arm.

"No, don't. Come back with me."

My head spun, and I felt dizzy. Images darted through my head, the shallow grave I inexplicably discovered, the people who came and went, the questions, the implications, the accusations.

"Come on," I heard Ollie's words urging me forward. I walked, but I didn't remember anything.

The air in the locker room hung thick with tension. Ollie sat me down and I slumped over. Every member of the team crowded around, concern etched on their faces.

I waved my hand. "Stop it. I'm fine," I grunted as I pulled myself to sit upright.

"Not even a little bit," Ollie said, placing her

hand firmly on my shoulder and pushing me back down.

Gabby reinforced her movement as she settled on my chest. Despite her very light weight, I felt her insistence and did as I was directed. I laid there.

Dr. Wright's words from earlier echoed in my head. Could she really know who killed Sophie? And if so, why hadn't she said anything sooner? That was the very question every member of the team blurted out when they heard what Wright said. And that was the moment Ollie began running to where we were meeting.

I smiled and held Ollie's hand. "Thanks, sis."

"Hey, if you're okay, we've got a lot of footage to review. We'll let you know what we find, okay?" Tyler was eager to get back to work, and I was more than happy to send them all away.

"Go! Work. Let's figure this out." I did my best rallying the troops voice and waved my fingers in the air.

Ollie didn't budge.

"Okay, what did you see?" She asked when it was just Gabby and us.

She was right. The entire walk to the meeting room was a blur because I was actually seeing something completely different.

I told Ollie what I'd seen and felt. Then I added, "Dr. Wright was there. I saw her at Sophie's grave."

"I've got some interesting anomalies here," Leo called out. "The jock ghosts might not be the only ones causing trouble. Look at this."

He played a clip of the upper stands, showing faint, glowing orbs zipping erratically across the screen. At first, they seemed harmless, playful even, but one shot toward the camera with enough force to knock it askew.

"Watch how erratic they are. Like they're running from something," Emily whispered.

Gabby squawked. "Danger! Danger!"

I tried to lift my head as I ran a hand down her back. "What is it, Gabby?"

Her head swiveled to the footage. She fluffed her feathers in agitation and let out a low whistle. "Run."

"Run from what?" Ollie asked softly.

"Wright."

I appreciated Gabby's warning, but running from Wright was the exact opposite of what I was going to do. I pled my case to the team.

"I'm going after her," I said. "She is as human as I am. She's even older and smaller than me. What's she going to do?"

"Bring a gun," Ollie said.

"Bring backup," Leo said.

"Use a knife," Emily added.

Tyler only motioned to the three of them and shrugged.

Then Ollie blurted out that I'd seen Wright at my sister's grave in a vision. Everyone wanted every detail, and I filled them in as much as I could.

"It wasn't very clear. I saw the grave like I saw it the first time, but this time, I also saw Wright. Much younger. Just standing there. She wasn't actually doing anything. Maybe investigating or something." I tried to find a reason for seeing her, but not Kaleb Smith.

As I struggled to convince myself and the group that everything was still okay, it was decided, without my input, that no one was to meet with Smith or Wright alone.

Which meant I was going to have to sneak away.

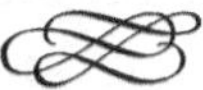

CHAPTER 10

Late that night, I crept out of bed and began feeling my way through the underground. After the visions I'd experienced earlier, my spidey sense was tingling, and I knew exactly where to go.

She was standing near the edge of the field. The floodlights cast long, dramatic shadows, and she seemed to relish the theater of it all. Her hands were clasped behind her back as she surveyed the space, an enigmatic smile curling her lips.

"You're working late," I said, announcing my presence.

She turned, her expression as smooth as glass. "So are you."

We stood in silence for a moment, the vast emptiness of the stadium amplifying the distance between us. Finally, I said, "You know who killed Sophie because you were there."

Wright tilted her head, considering me with an expression that was both patient and patronizing.

"Well done." Then she stepped closer, her tone softening to something almost maternal. "You know, I've been where you are. Rejected, outcast, blamed for things I had no control over."

"What are you really doing here, Margo?"

Her smile froze in place, but her eyes darkened. "I could ask you the same thing, *Jackie*. You've been playing a dangerous game. Poking around in things you don't understand."

"Then why don't you enlighten me?" I shot back, my fear giving way to anger.

"That's exactly what I intend to do."

I stared in shock as she pulled out a gun and aimed it at me.

"Don't move," her voice was calm, almost conversational.

"What are you doing? Have you lost your mind?"

"I've lost a lot of things in this life, but I can assure you, my mind is not one of them. Now, turn around. Slowly."

I complied, raising my hands as I turned away

from her and stared into the dark hallway ahead of me.

"Start walking," she commanded.

"Where are we going?" I asked, my voice trembling despite my efforts to sound calm.

"Under the stadium," she replied. "To get answers once and for all. For both of us."

The hallway narrowed and descended further down than I thought possible. Soon we were moving down a steep set of stairs. Each step echoed ominously, the sound swallowed quickly by the oppressive darkness below.

At the bottom of the stairs, the air was colder, heavier. The faint hum of energy I'd felt throughout the stadium was stronger here, vibrating in my chest like a second heartbeat. Wright pushed me forward into a large, open chamber.

Kaleb Smith was waiting. His spectral form was even sharper than before and his eyes gleamed with a predatory intelligence as they locked onto mine.

"Welcome," he said, his voice like the scrape of metal against stone. "It's good to see you again. Without your friends listening in and interfering, that is."

I swallowed hard, my throat dry. "I wish I could say the same."

He chuckled, a low, menacing sound.

"What is this?" I demanded, my voice steadier than I felt. "What do you want from me?"

Kaleb stepped closer, his translucent figure casting an eerie glow on the walls. "You've been looking for answers, Margo and I, we, think it's finally time to give them to you."

I turned to Wright, anger flaring in my chest. "What's your role in all this? Why are you so invested in this?"

Wright's smile was razor thin. "I made a promise, Jackie. A promise to someone I loved. To someone who says he loves me."

As she spoke, Smith moved closer to her and put his arm around her shoulders. Somehow, they kissed as my stomach churned and the pieces fell into place.

"You knew him before you came here?" I said, as the realization hit me like a freight train.

"I've known him forever," she said. "I'm the only one who ever really understood him." Her voice softened as she looked into his black eyes. "Kaleb was more than the monster they painted him to be. He was a man—flawed, yes, but misunderstood."

"Misunderstood?" I spat. "He was a killer!"

"Ah, so quick to judge," Kaleb interjected, his tone mocking. "But tell me, Jackie, what would you do to protect someone you loved? To avenge them?"

"Don't," I snapped. "Don't try to compare us. I would never—"

"And yet, here you are doing that very thing. Playing god. Accusing someone who is innocent," Wright hissed.

"How do you know he's innocent?" I asked. "You were there. You had to have witnessed it! How can you say he's innocent?"

Wright hesitated, her mouth in a perfect O, then she smiled.

"Go on, tell her," Kaleb Smith was bouncing on his ghostly toes. "Tell her what you did!"

My blood ran cold, and I turned to her. "Tell me. What? Did you help him? Did you watch?"

"Enough," Wright interrupted, her voice sharp again. "This isn't about what I did or didn't do. It's about what's coming. What's owed to me for my dedication."

I stared at her, my heart pounding. "It's absolutely about what you did. Tell me! Tell me now!"

She only laughed.

Why was she torturing me like this? What was the point?

"Tie her up, darling," Wright said. "We've got a plan to put into place."

"What plan?" I demanded.

Kaleb's smile widened, his spectral form seeming to grow darker, more menacing. "To finish what we started. To leave a mark so indelible, it will echo through eternity. To cause the ultimate destruction."

My breath caught in my throat. "You're going to destroy the stadium."

Wright nodded, her expression almost serene. "And with it, we'll finally be free. Together."

"You're insane," I whispered, taking a step back.

She grabbed my arms and wrenched them behind me. Soon my hands were tied. As she worked, she muttered to herself.

"Am I insane? Well, maybe. I mean there were some signs. Or maybe you're just too blind to see the truth. This place is a prison. For him, for me, for all the souls trapped here. We're simply breaking the chains. How is that insane? It's helping."

"What about the innocent people involved? You're not helping. You're harming innocent people!"

"They're collateral," Kaleb said coldly. "Necessary sacrifices. Just like your precious Sophie."

I shook my head, bile rising in my throat. "No! No, you can't"

"Don't worry. You won't have to watch."

Kaleb stepped closer, his spectral hand reaching out toward me. The air grew colder. The room spun around me. My vision blurred as his icy touch closed around my arm.

And then everything went black.

I woke up to the sound of muffled voices and the faint hum of equipment. My wrists ached from the ropes Wright had used, though they were now untied. Slowly, I realized I was lying on the floor of the women's locker room once again. My head throbbed, and as I pushed myself up, I saw the team gathered around, their faces etched with worry...again.

"Jackie!" Emily was the first to rush over, helping me sit upright. "Thank goodness you're awake!"

"Where's Wright?" I croaked, my throat dry. "And Kaleb Smith?"

"They're gone," Tyler said, his voice grim. "But you're safe now."

"No!" I grabbed Emily's arm. "You don't understand—they're going to blow up the stadium. Everyone here is in danger!"

Gabby fluttered to my shoulder, her usual sass replaced by a soothing coo. "Safe now," she murmured.

"No, listen!" I said, my voice rising. "They're planning something big. We need to get everyone out of here."

Ollie crouched beside me, her expression calm but firm. "Jackie, listen to us. We know."

"What?" I blinked at her, confused. "How?"

Ollie exchanged a glance with Tyler, who nodded. "We found something," Tyler said. "After you disappeared, we followed some leads... and Wright slipped up."

"Slipped up how?" My heart pounded as I waited for his answer.

"She left her notebook," Emily said. "Leo found it along the edge of the field where you were last seen. When we woke up and you weren't here, we pulled up the footage and saw Wright lead you away. When we went there to follow you, we found it."

"Let me see." My hands trembled as I reached out.

"The police have it. It's evidence. But we took pictures before we called them. Here."

Emily held out her phone, and I squinted at the tiny print.

"I got you," Ollie said. She opened her laptop and then handed me my glasses. Now I could actually see.

I scanned through various images showing detailed sketches of the stadium's layout, notes on its structural weaknesses, and plans for a "grand finale." Chillingly, the words "for Kaleb" were scrawled repeatedly in the margins.

"She's completely unhinged," I whispered. "This is evidence of everything."

"That's not all," Emily said. She reached around me and pulled up a video. "After you were taken, Tyler set up a hidden camera near the underpass. Look."

The screen showed Wright pacing beneath the stadium. Her face twisted with anger as she spoke to someone off-camera. "This place will be our redemption," she hissed. "You will be remembered forever."

Then a deep, menacing voice echoed through

the clip. "Wait until the stadium is full, Lydia. Maximum impact."

"Of course. I know that!" The video cut out as Wright stormed out of the frame.

"Lydia?" I repeated, stunned.

Ollie nodded. "It's the name of the woman who visited him in prison all those years. Lydia Grant changed her name to Margo Wright. They've been planning this for years."

I struggled to my feet, the pieces clicking into place.

"They are partners," I whispered.

"She changed her name so she could hide who she really was. It wasn't suspicious for Dr. Margo Wright to be investigating his case. Or for her to be interested in his remains. But if Lydia, Wright's girlfriend, was doing those things, that would raise questions," Emily said.

"Lydia Grant was questioned as part of one of the investigations. She was a person of interest, but they couldn't find anything concrete. Then, she seemed to just disappear," Ollie said.

"They were partners," I said again. "She knows who killed Sophie because she was there when it happened."

"And now they are partnering up again to finish what they started," Tyler added grimly.

"Or what Kaleb wanted," Emily said. "That 'blaze of glory' Wright mentioned."

"They are going to do it during the game," I said, my voice barely above a whisper. "We have to stop them."

"They were going to do it during the game," Tyler said. "But Wright was arrested. Um...," he hesitated and looked at Ollie.

"I'll tell her," Ollie said. "Give us a moment, okay?"

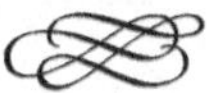

Ollie's voice cut through the tense silence in the locker room as she turned to face me, her expression somber. "Jackie, there's a little bit more that I need to tell you. This won't be easy."

I had been pacing, restless energy coursing through me as I tried to make sense of Kaleb Smith's words and the fractured pieces of the investigation. Ollie's serious tone brought me to a halt.

"What is it?" I asked, my heart pounding. "What could be worse than this?"

Ollie exchanged a glance with Emily, who sat at the table, her tablet glowing with open files. Emily nodded subtly, encouraging Ollie to continue.

"I don't know how else to say this," Ollie began,

her hands wringing nervously. "But we've been digging into Margo Wright a little more. Actually digging into her real name, Lydia Grant. And, well...we think she's the one who killed Sophie."

Her words hit me like a physical blow. I staggered back, shaking my head as if denying it would make it untrue. "No. That's impossible. Why would she—how could she?"

Emily spoke up, her voice steady but heavy. "We found out more about her history, Jackie. She and Kaleb Smith have a connection that goes way back—high school, in fact."

"High school?" I repeated, stunned.

"Yes," Emily confirmed. "She was his first girl-friend, and according to what we've pieced together, they stayed in touch even after he started his killing spree. When he was in prison, she visited him regularly. Her name even appears on visitor logs from his final years."

"That doesn't prove anything," I said, though my voice wavered. "She could have been trying to reform him or—"

Emily held up a hand. "It's more than that. Her history shows a pattern of instability. Wright was expelled from two universities before finally earning her degree—both incidents involved violent outbursts. And her thesis, written years after Kaleb's conviction, centered on society's 'misjudgment' of serial killers and even suggests that they serve a role and purpose in society."

Ollie chimed in. "She's obsessed with him, Jackie. Everything in her life has been about Kaleb—understanding him, defending him, doing his bidding, and now carrying out whatever twisted plans they made together."

I slumped into a chair, my mind racing. "But why Sophie? What did she have to do with this?"

Ollie hesitated before answering, her voice soft. "We think Sophie was in the wrong place at the wrong time. Wright was in your town during the year Sophie disappeared. Emily found records of a lecture she gave at the university nearby, just weeks before..."

"She killed her," I finished, my voice breaking. The weight of the revelation threatened to crush me. "Why didn't the police make the connection?"

"They did, and they questioned her as Lydia Grant. But then she changed her name and disappeared. We think she was the connection they would have needed to Smith, or Smith was the connection they needed to her. Either way, once she disappeared, he was charged for the other murders, but not Sophie's."

I buried my face in my hands, struggling to

process the information. "All this time," I whispered. "I thought it might be Kaleb, but it was her. She's been right here this whole time."

Ollie placed a comforting hand on my shoulder. "We didn't know then, but we know now. The police already have her in custody for the notebook. They found explosives and the gun on her as well. We will share everything with them and it won't be difficult to draw the connections. She won't get away with it any longer."

The team regrouped while I stayed behind with Emily, poring over the files she had uncovered. The pieces of Wright's life painted a disturbing picture—one of a woman who had dedicated herself to Kaleb Smith's legacy, even after his death. Her visits to the prison, her involvement in academic studies on criminal psychology, and her eventual arrival at the university all pointed to a chilling conclusion. She had orchestrated this from the beginning.

"Do we know what the endgame is now that Wright's been arrested?" I asked Emily.

She shook her head. "That's what the rest of the team is working on. Based on what we've learned, it's possible Smith will continue with the plan. He might not need Wright at all. And honestly, that's what she was most afraid of. I think she needed to prove to him she was valuable to him. Sophie was a way for her to prove her loyalty. And this," Emily motioned to the stadium above us, "is her ultimate gesture."

I leaned back, the weight of the revelation pressing down on me. "She said she knew who killed Sophie. She wasn't lying. She just didn't tell me it was her."

Emily reached out, squeezing my hand. "We're going to figure this out, Jackie. Together."

"I know. And I don't have time to sit around feeling sorry for myself, do I? There's a game tonight and as of now, Smith is still running around here. If the ghost jocks can manipulate the players during a game, who's to say Smith can't do the same? He might not need Wright, but he has plenty of other options, right?"

Emily snapped her laptop shut. "Let's go!"

CHAPTER 12

We worked hard throughout the afternoon juggling the police and the FBI, both of whom were very interested in what Wright may have planned for the stadium. Dogs were brought in to sniff for explosives while other agents searched every nook and cranny of the stadium.

After an exhaustive search from them and extensive questioning of Wright, it was determined there was nothing dangerous, and the stadium was safe for the game that night.

While the school officials were satisfied and everyone breathed a sigh of relief that the game could go on, my team and I were in a panic.

"We should say something," Tyler kept saying.

"Like what?" Ollie would ask. "We know you swept the place and have declared it safe, but you didn't account for the psychopathic ghost bent on destruction that may or may not be able to manipulate solid objects and may or may not be planning to destroy everything?"

She didn't say this to be cruel or snarky, even though it came across that way. Knowing her as I did, she was expressing her own frustration at not knowing how to move forward. And she was right. What were we supposed to say? And there was no way they would cancel the game because a TV show about haunted places said to.

Instead, we did what we did best. We planned, and we took action.

Ollie and Leo set up their gear and positioned themselves in the lower tunnels, while Tyler and Emily set up near the field. I stayed standing in the back of the press box, with promises to stay out of the way and to stay quiet, with Gabby perched on my shoulder. Her occasional whistles and muttered warnings did little to ease my nerves.

Hours passed with no significant activity beyond the game itself. Just as I was thinking the night would be uneventful, and we had disabled Smith's plan, Tyler's voice crackled over the radio.

"Jackie, we've got movement near the southeast corner," he said. "It looks like someone's down there."

"Is it Smith?" I asked, my heart racing.

"I'm not sure," he replied.

"I'm on my way," I said, already heading for the stairs.

Gabby squawked, her voice urgent. "Danger! Danger!"

I quietly left the press box and made my way to the southeast corner of the stadium. The bright lights and crowd noise followed me a few yards into the tunnel and then it grew dark. This wasn't an area they used often, and it was mostly empty.

"Where are you?" I whispered. "Tyler?"

He didn't reply and I couldn't see him anywhere. I continued to make my way further into the tunnels. The air grew colder, the oppressive energy pressing against me like a physical weight. My flashlight flickered, the beam struggling to penetrate the darkness.

The air beneath the stadium was suffocating. The weight of its silence pressed down on me when I turned a corner and stood face to face with Kaleb Smith. His spectral form flickered like a half-remembered nightmare. My pulse pounded in my ears and Gabby shifted uneasily on my shoulder, her claws digging in just enough to ground me.

"Jackie," Kaleb said, his voice low and slow, like a predator toying with prey. "You've come a long way for this."

"For answers," I corrected, forcing steel into my voice. "And justice. But you wouldn't know anything about that."

"Justice," he repeated, a bitter chuckle escaping him. "Is that what you think this is about? You're chasing ghosts, Jackie. You know by now that I didn't kill Sophie."

"But you were there." The words came out more like a challenge than a statement. My throat felt dry, each syllable scraping against it like sandpaper.

His expression shifted, the faint smirk vanishing as he stepped closer. His eyes—dull, gray orbs with the weight of the grave behind them —locked onto mine. "Yes," he said. "I was there."

Kaleb's voice softened, his tone almost pitying. "But I didn't touch her, Jackie. I swear that to you."

"That's not good enough!" I shouted, the room spinning around me. "You expect me to believe you stood by while someone else - while Wright did that? And she did it for you? You could have stopped her!"

"No, I couldn't stop her. She was obsessed with me. Always has been. I didn't ask her to kill Sophie, but she thought it would prove her loyalty. That it would make me... love her."

"No." My head shook before I even realized I was doing it. "That doesn't make sense. Sophie had nothing to do with you. Why would Wright—"

"It didn't matter who," Kaleb interrupted. "Anyone would have done. She was simply convinced that this was the way to show her loyalty and win my affections."

"She killed my sister to make you love her."

"Yes, it would appear so," Kaleb said. "To please me. To show me how far she would go for me, for my love."

A cold rage built in my chest, spreading outward until it reached my fingers, trembling with the need to strike something—anything. "And what did you do, Kaleb?" I demanded. "Did you thank her? Tell her she'd done a good job?"

His expression darkened, the edges of his form flickering. "I told her she was a fool."

"Not good enough," I said through gritted teeth. "You could have stopped her. You could have—"

"I was no match for her delusions. Whatever you think of me, she was worse."

"Maybe, but you didn't help. You fed her delusions," I shot back, my voice breaking. "You're just as responsible as she is. You manipulated her, and she destroyed my family because of it."

Kaleb stepped closer, his form towering over me now. "I didn't manipulate her, Jackie. She acted on her own. And now I want to finish this once and for all. If you want this to end, I need your help." His voice grew quieter now, almost pleading. "I told you all of this because you deserve to know the truth. And because I need you."

I shook my head, tears burning at the edges of my vision. "You need me? Ha! I'm not doing anything for you. Why should I believe anything you're saying?"

"Because I know what's coming," he said, his voice hollow now. "The plan is already in motion. I just need someone living to strike a match. Help me and we will all win. You will have revenge for Sophie. Lydia won't get what she's wanted all along. It will be you instead. You who gets to leave your mark, not her. You who gets the glory. Help me Jackie," Kaleb said, his tone softening again. "If not for me, then for Sophie."

"Don't you dare use her name," I said, venom lacing my words. "You don't get to use my sister as leverage."

"Then do it for yourself," he pressed. "Do it for all the times you weren't enough. Do it for the blame you felt every time someone mentioned her name. Do it to take away from Sophie's killer the one thing she wants more than anything."

My mind whirled, torn between rage and confusion as I fought to steady my breathing. This was insane. I knew it. But why were his words making sense? Why was I even here, still considering what he was saying?

And then Gabby's voice, sharp and clear, cut through the fog. "Liar. It's a trap," she said, her tone insistent now. "Don't."

Kaleb's form flickered again, and for the first time, I saw the cracks in his facade. The desperation lurking beneath his calm exterior.

That was enough for me.

Gabby whispered into my ear. "Walk away. Walk away now. You know what is right. He's messing with your head. Walk away."

Without another word, I turned and walked away from Kaleb Smith.

As soon as I was out of his sight, I ran.

"Faster," Gabby whispered, flapping her wings as though to help me move quicker.

"Anyone there?" I yelled into my headset. "Anyone?"

I only heard static and pops, but I kept trying.

"Anyone hearing me? He needs help," I said through heavy breaths. "He needs someone to literally strike a match for him."

"Where are you?" Emily's voice broke through.

"Oh, thank goodness!" I said. "Coming out on the southeast corner right now."

I squinted as I broke out of the bleak darkness of the tunnel into the bright lights of the game and right into Tyler.

He caught me easily and steadied me as Gabby fluttered just above us. By the time we settled, the rest of the team arrived looking just as flustered as I felt.

"He needs help," I gasped to the group.

"Then we just make sure he doesn't get the help," Emily said. "Easy enough. We don't help him."

"It might not be that easy. Guys...look," Leo pointed to his monitor.

We clearly saw Kaleb Smith standing in the middle of the field as the game continued around him.

"What's he doing?" Ollie whispered.

"Trying to get help," I said.

"The ghost jocks. He's trying to get their help. Watch."

Ollie pointed to the field, and we all looked up from the monitor. Smith was towering over the rest of the ghosts as they mingled with the actual living players. He was ruining their fun. Still, eventually, every one of them stopped and listened to him as the game continued around them.

"How do we stop this? Can we stop this?"

"Yes," I nodded. "Yes, we can."

"How?"

"Ghosts don't hold absolute power. They're bound by their connections—places, people, objects," I reminded the group. "Smith is tied to this stadium, to his remains. If we can disrupt those ties, we weaken him."

"But we don't know where his remains are, right? Are they at the Body Farm still?" Emily asked.

"No, I don't think so. Remember, Wright didn't even know where they were," Leo added.

I hesitated, then looked at Ollie. "We're not alone in this. Harry, Martin, Terrance, those ghosts have power too. If we can convince them to help us, we stand a chance."

"It's not like we have another option," Ollie said. "We need to try."

The plan took shape quickly. Tyler and Emily would try to get the attention of the ghost jocks on the field while Ollie and Leo sought Harry, Martin, and Terrance in the tunnels.

As everyone separated, Ollie stopped me. "Jackie? What are you going to do?"

I shook my head. "I don't know. I feel useless right now. I'm numb, and it's like my mind isn't working."

Ollie nodded wisely. "I have a suggestion."

I looked at her expectantly. "Go on."

"Focus. Focus on only one thing. What are you good at, Jackie? What can you do right now that no one else can do?"

I shook my head at Ollie. What in the world was she talking about? I couldn't do anything other than almost get us all killed and feel sorry for myself.

Then Gabby whispered to me again.

In a voice that sounded so much like my grandmother, Gabby reminded me of my unique psychic abilities.

"Ollie's right," she said. "Focus. What do you need right now? It will be okay."

The stadium was eerily quiet as we split up, the only sounds the hum of equipment and the occasional creak of old metal. I wandered the halls of the old forensic anthropology department.

"What we need are his bones," I murmured, my voice trembling slightly. "But where?"

"Focus," Gabby said helpfully.

"Yeah, I'm trying Gabs. Any ideas? Are they in the middle of the Body Farm? Or tucked away somewhere under the stadium. How in the world do I find them?"

I felt like I was wandering aimlessly back and forth along the same hallway, but I must have had some sort of instinct because in time, I ended up in front of the same snack machine where the mysterious ghost had walked through me earlier. I stood in front of the machine and within a few seconds, he appeared again.

"Hey!" I waved my hand in front of him. "I think you're supposed to help me! Come on, I know you can see me!" I was jumping up and down by now, Gabby flapping her wings with each mini updraft. "Dude! Come on!"

He ignored me just as before and even turned

towards me. Looking through me, he moved forward. I jumped out of his way just in time before he passed through me again. I didn't have the energy for that.

But I did have the energy to follow him. He didn't disappear like so many of the others did . Instead, he shuffled down the hallway with me right on his heels. He turned a few corners and eventually entered a small office, where he sat at a small desk with a clipboard and a pencil. I debated trying to get his attention again, but was just about to give up.

"Can I help you?"

I screamed and spun around.

Behind me, in a dark corner of the room, sat a young woman.

"Hi, I'm Jackie," I said. "I hope you can help. I'm here because of Kaleb Smith and Dr. Wright. Do you know them?"

The figure stood and nodded. "Yes, of course. I've been assisting Professor McAlister with some data regarding them. They are very bad people, you know?"

"Yes, I know. I'm glad you can see me. Is that Professor McAlister?" I motioned to the man at the other desk.

She nodded. "Yes, he won't talk to you, though. He's very smart and very busy. I will try to help you. I'm Betsy Flanagan, his research assistant." She lowered her voice and giggled. "Between you and me, I probably know more than he does."

"Thank you. I really appreciate that." I smiled.

"Of course. What do you need?" She asked as she stood and smoothed the front of her pencil skirt.

"I need to find Kaleb Smith's remains. I don't know if they are here, or at the -"

My words died when she turned her back. The entire back of her head was gone. Hair hung down each side of the gaping wound. My heart fell into my stomach and I felt like I'd vomit.

"Follow me," she said. "I've kept up with his remains and I've been watching Lydia Grant from the moment she stepped foot into the building. Here we go." She threw open a hidden door. One entire wall was full of drawers with fading labels on them. Betsy went straight to the one on the end and pointed. "I can't open it, but you can."

I crouched down and, with shaking fingers, brushed the dust from the label. It read "Kaleb Smith - remains."

I opened the drawer to the only physical remains of Smith. His skull, and what seemed to be most of his torso. I gathered everything into my arms and looked for something to carry them.

Betsy pointed to a canvas bag sitting in the corner.

"This is perfect! Thank you! I have to go," I said to her as I stuffed the bones into the bag. "This is amazing. This will set all the ghosts here free. Including you! Thank you, you are a hero."

Betsy smiled and waved me off. "My pleasure. It's been long overdue, actually."

I hesitated, wanting to ask her what happened to her but not wanting to be rude. Instead, I said, "You said you've been keeping tabs on Smith and Wright, or I guess you knew her as Lydia Grant. How do you know them?"

Betsy turned back to me and smiled. "They are my murderers."

TYLER REED: TAKE 3

The camera opens with a low shot of the shadowy stadium corridors, the air heavy with dampness and an eerie stillness. Tyler Reed steps into frame, his usual confidence tempered by the weight of the mystery surrounding Smoky Stadium.

"Welcome back to *Haunted Histories*," he begins, his voice steady but laced with tension. "I'm Tyler Reed, and tonight we return to Smoky Stadium. What was once a place of roaring crowds and triumphant cheers has become a labyrinth of secrets and restless spirits. But as we've discovered, the dead aren't the only ones keeping secrets."

The shot transitions to the team—Jackie, Ollie, Emily, and Leo—moving cautiously through dimly lit tunnels. Their flashlights slice through the darkness, casting fleeting shadows that seem to dance on the walls.

"Our investigation has uncovered more questions than answers," Tyler continues in a voiceover. "Beneath this stadium lies a history of science and tragedy, where classrooms once studied the decomposition of the human body and the spirits of those used for research now linger. But even these ghosts are hesitant to speak freely, warning us of a greater danger that may lie ahead."

The camera cuts to Tyler, now standing in the field's empty bleachers, overlooking the vast and silent stadium. "What we've learned so far paints a chilling picture: a campus haunted not only by the spirits of the dead but perhaps by the ambitions of the living. Dr. Wright's connection to these events remains unclear, but her influence seems to reach far deeper than we initially believed."

Tyler steps forward, his tone sharpening with resolve. "And then there's Kaleb Smith, the notorious serial killer whose remains are rumored to rest here, disturbed by the renovations. His presence—whether as a restless spirit or a symbol of unresolved justice—casts a long shadow over this investigation. Is he tied to the escalating disturbances, or is he another piece of a much larger puzzle?"

"As our investigation deepens, one thing is clear: the stakes are higher than ever. The spirits here hold the keys to a truth long buried, but unlocking it will require confronting not just the dead, but the secrets they've taken to their graves."

The camera pans out, capturing the vast emptiness of the stadium, the shadows stretching long across the field. Tyler's voice carries over the haunting image: "Stay with us as we navigate the fine line between the living and the dead, and uncover the true story hidden beneath Smoky Stadium."

Fade to black.

CHAPTER 14

As I ran towards the field and got closer to the signal, I started hearing voices crackling in my earpiece again.

Tyler's voice came through, breathless but excited. "We've got them! The jocks are on board."

"We're close to convincing Harry and the crew. Stand by." Ollie's voice crackled right after Tyler's.

I reached Tyler and Emily on the field first. They had gotten the attention of two of the jocks and were explaining to them what was happening.

"That guy?" one of them asked, pointing at Kaleb. "He's the big bad?"

Tyler nodded.

"Yeah, happy to help you out, buddy. He's a menace. Always messing with our games."

"Focus," I said, trying to keep their energy

contained. "We need your help to stop him. This is very serious."

"Relax," another jock said, spinning a phantom football on his finger. "We've got this."

Moments later, Harry, Martin, and Terrance appeared, their forms glowing faintly in the moonlight. "Looks like we're late to the party," Harry quipped.

"Glad you're here," I said, relief evident in my voice. "We need all the help we can get."

Ollie and Leo arrived shortly after. The team huddled in a far corner of the field while the game continued. The ghosts were finished with us and immediately went onto the field, ready to fight.

"Do they know what to do?" I fretted. "We didn't really tell them anything."

"I think they've got it," Ollie said. "We can watch here."

"Why are we watching monitors?" I asked. "Let's get closer. Maybe we can help."

"We can't. They won't let us. Security stopped us last time when we were trying to get their attention," Emily said.

I frowned and thought for a few moments, then snapped my fingers. "The first guy we met, what was his name?"

"Jason, Jason Stewart," Emily almost shouted with glee. "I've got his number."

Even in all the chaos of the moment, I couldn't help but notice Leo's sideways glance when she said that.

A quick call to our friend Jason and in no time, we were being fitted with VIP lanyards and escorted to the sidelines.

"Just stay back here," Jason begged. "It's bad enough as it is. The players keep tripping and falling down. I don't know what's going on suddenly. The mood is pretty ugly."

We told him we'd stay put, but to our trained eyes, we could easily see what was actually happening on the field. The ghosts were lining up, completely ignoring the other actual living players. And they were attempting to tackle Kaleb Smith.

"Looks like someone's messing with our field," one of them said, his voice a deep rumble.

"Not on our watch," another added, cracking his ghostly knuckles.

Kaleb turned toward them, his form rippling with anger. "Stay out of this!" he roared.

But the football ghosts weren't deterred. "This is our turf," the leader said firmly. "You've overstayed your welcome, Kaleb."

As they advanced, the surrounding air seemed

to shift, pushing back the oppressive weight of his presence. The tendrils of mist recoiled, retreating toward their source. Smith snarled, his shadowy form flickering as if struggling to maintain its shape.

From the sidelines, three more figures emerged—Harry, Martin, and Terrance. The trio of spectral pranksters hovered hesitantly before exchanging glances and nodding.

"We've got your back," Harry called to the football ghosts. "Let's show him what teamwork looks like."

The six ghosts formed a line, their combined energy crackling in the air. The stadium seemed to hum with their collective power, the floodlights surging back to life in brilliant defiance.

My heart pounded as the spectral showdown unfolded. Smith launched himself at the football ghosts, his tendrils lashing out like whips. But the jocks stood their ground, blocking his attacks with spectral shields that shimmered like invisible walls.

Harry and his crew darted around the edges of the battlefield, their prankster instincts turning the fight into a chaotic whirlwind. They tripped Smith with phantom footballs, redirected his attacks with clever misdirection, and even disoriented him with bursts of blinding light.

Smith roared in frustration, his form growing increasingly unstable. "You cannot defeat me!" he bellowed, his voice reverberating through the stadium. "I am eternal!"

"Not tonight," the leader of the football ghosts replied. With a final surge of energy, he and his teammates charged forward, their combined force colliding with Smith in an explosion of light and sound.

The air grew heavier as his form expanded, the mist around him swirling violently. Somehow, his black eyes found me and he sneered. "You think these fools can stop me?"

"They're not fools," I shot back. "And neither am I."

Gabby squawked loudly, her feathers bristling as she took flight, circling above us like a guardian. She cried. "Strike now!"

At her cue, the ghosts launched their assault. The prankster jocks darted around Kaleb, their speed creating whirlwinds that disrupted his misty form. Harry, Martin, and Terrance focused their energy into bursts of light, each one striking

Smith with a force that made him flicker and falter.

Their actions were visible only to us and for the actual players, it appeared as though the ball had a mind of its own. The whirlwinds moved the ball erratically around the field and the electrical impulses from the lights seemed to confuse the players as they stumbled blindly in all directions.

I stayed back, watching in awe as the spectral battle unfolded. Kaleb fought back fiercely, his tendrils of mist lashing out and striking some of the ghosts, sending them reeling. But they regrouped quickly, their unity giving them strength.

Kaleb's form shimmered in and out of focus, a grotesque mix of shadow and mist that moved with an unnatural fluidity. He loomed over us at the center of the field, his voice cold and jagged.

"No one leaves," Kaleb declared, his words laced with malice that echoed across the stadium. The air grew thick, heavy with a pressure that made every breath feel like a struggle. The floodlights dimmed, their glow flickering erratically as if the electricity itself was afraid of him.

Kaleb's laughter boomed across the field, low and guttural. "You came here seeking answers," he said, his voice a thunderous growl. "But you'll leave with nothing." His threat was directed towards me.

The crowd grew silent, as though they sensed something was happening. Even the players themselves grew quiet and still. The referees calling an official timeout while they reviewed footage and someone said to get the parrot off the field.

Ollie was listening to the game through her headset and said the announcers were commenting about some type of weather anomaly. They considered evacuating the stadium.

The surrounding mist thickened, curling outward like tendrils. The field itself seemed to shift beneath our feet, the grass cold and damp as though soaked in dew despite the warm night air. Suddenly, those tendrils shot out, snaking toward us like spectral chains.

"Move!" I yelled, yanking Emily to the side just as one of the ghostly appendages lashed out, striking the ground where she'd stood.

Ollie stumbled back, her sound equipment clattering to the turf. Leo grabbed her arm, pulling her to safety as another tendril narrowly missed them. Tyler tripped over his own feet in his rush to avoid a third strike.

"We can't outrun him," Ollie panted, her face pale. "He's everywhere! Jackie, do something!"

The impact sent a shockwave across the field, knocking us to the ground.

"You can't stop me," he bellowed, as he battled the ghost players who had him surrounded.

"I can't on my own, but I have help. And I have this!" I replied, holding up the bag containing his bones. "You're not invincible, Kaleb. And you're not as strong as you think."

He smirked, his form shifting slightly, as if testing his limits. "Bold words for someone so fragile."

Gabby landed on my shoulder, her voice urgent. "It's time. Help them," she whispered.

"What do I do?"

"Focus," she said, her tone firm. "Your power. Use it."

I closed my eyes, taking a deep breath. Clara's teachings and my Grandmother's words echoed in my mind—harness your energy, channel it. I reached out, my hands trembling as I focused on the connection I felt to this place, to the ghosts fighting for me, for the spirit of my sister.

A surge of warmth spread through me, and when I opened my eyes, a faint glow surrounded my hands. Gabby let out a triumphant squawk. "Yes!"

I raised my hands, directing the energy toward Kaleb. The glow shot forward, colliding with him and forcing him to stumble back. The other ghosts seized the opportunity, their combined power overwhelming him.

While he was fighting for the upper hand, I reached into the bag and withdrew his skeleton. Kaleb let out a furious roar as his form faded in and out. "This isn't over, Jackie!" he bellowed.

With my glowing fingers, I pulled the skull out. Before I knew what was happening, the prankster jocks grabbed it and began playing football with it. Within seconds, Kaleb Smith's skeletal head was sailing through the uprights.

While the ghosts cheered, the form of Kaleb was fading quickly. Other ghosts picked various parts of his skeleton up and carried them to other parts of the field.

Soon he was almost invisible, his voice a whisper. With a final gasp, followed by a loud cheer, what was left of Kaleb Smith disappeared into the air.

Silence fell over the stadium, broken only by the soft hum of our equipment.

Suddenly, the band began to play and everyone

came back alive. It was as though nothing out of the ordinary had happened.

"The announcers are saying there was some weird weather occurrence, and the game is going on as scheduled." Ollie shrugged.

The ghosts made their way to where we were standing.

"Nice work," Harry said with a nod. "Didn't think you had it in you."

"Neither did I," I admitted, my voice shaky. "You guys did a good job too."

Gabby nuzzled my cheek, her warmth soothing the tension in my chest. "Good job," she whispered.

As the ghosts began to fade, their forms flickered like fading stars. I felt a sense of peace settle over the field.

As we watched, the home team scored a touchdown. Amid the orange fireworks and light show celebrating the score, we could see the misty forms of what had to be dozens of ghosts raise above the stadium.

Only one remained.

Betsy Flanagan stood before me.

"Thank you," she said simply.

Then she, too, joined the others as they disappeared into the sky.

The stadium stood eerily still as dawn broke, the first rays of sunlight glinting off the steel beams and casting long shadows over the empty field. The oppressive energy that had lingered here for so long was gone, leaving behind a strange, almost hollow quiet. Kaleb Smith was vanquished, and Dr. Wright's dark secrets had been unearthed, but I couldn't shake the bittersweet ache that came with the finality of it all.

I stood at the edge of the field, Gabby perched on my shoulder, her feathers unusually subdued. "Done now," she murmured, almost as if she needed to convince herself.

"Yeah," I replied, my voice barely above a whisper. "It's done."

Behind me, the team was packing up the last of

our equipment. Leo's camera gear was neatly stowed in its case, and he was carefully coiling wires with the precision of someone who needed to keep his hands busy to stop his mind from racing. Emily, always the multitasker, was jotting down final notes on her tablet while chatting softly with Ollie, who had her sound recorder tucked under one arm.

I turned to face them, my heart swelling with gratitude for the people who had stuck by me through this twisted journey. "Everyone," I called out, my voice carrying across the field. "Can we gather for a minute?"

They approached, forming a loose circle around me, their expressions a mix of relief, exhaustion, and quiet triumph.

"I just wanted to say thank you," I began, glancing at each of them in turn. "This wasn't just another case. This was personal, and I know it pushed all of us to the edge. But we did it. We solved the mystery, we got the answers, and most importantly, we made it out together."

"Barely," Tyler muttered, though his grin took the sting out of his words.

Ollie placed a hand on my shoulder, her warmth grounding me. "You were amazing, Jackie.

And Gabby too. We couldn't have done this without you."

Gabby squawked, clearly pleased with the acknowledgment. "The best!" she proclaimed.

"Modest as ever," Leo quipped, earning a round of chuckles.

Emily stepped forward, her tablet clutched tightly. "I've been reviewing everything—the footage, the recordings, the notes. What we've captured here is groundbreaking, Jackie. This isn't just a great episode for the show. It's a story that matters. We can give Betsy Flanagan's family some peace now, knowing what happened to her."

"Yeah, I understand Dr. Wright is singing like a canary right now. No offense," Leo added, shooting a glance at Gabby.

His words hung in the air, resonating deeply. This wasn't just about the ghosts or the hauntings. This was about giving voice to the forgotten, uncovering truths that had been buried for too long.

"Let's make sure we tell it right," I said, a newfound resolve hardening in my chest. "Not just for the viewers, but for Sophie and for Betsy. For everyone who deserves to be remembered."

The mention of my sister brought a heavy pause, but it wasn't the suffocating grief I'd carried for so long. It felt lighter now, tempered by understanding and the knowledge that I'd finally taken a step toward justice.

Ollie broke the silence, her tone light but sincere. "So what's next, boss? Do we actually get a vacation this time, or is there another haunted library waiting for us?"

"Vacation sounds good," Tyler said quickly. "Somewhere with no ghosts. Or murders."

I smiled, the warmth of their camaraderie filling the hollow space that grief had left behind. "We'll see," I said. "But first, let's finish what we started here."

Later, as the team packed up the van, I found myself wandering back to the edge of the field. The stadium felt different now, no longer weighed down by its past. It was just a place—bricks and steel and history, like so many others.

Gabby fluttered to the ground in front of me, her black eyes gleaming with mischief. "Big plans?" she asked.

"Maybe," I replied, crouching down to meet her gaze. "But first, I need to go home. It's time to visit Sophie."

Gabby tilted her head, her beak clicking softly. "Good idea."

It was. For the first time in years, the thought of

visiting my sister's grave didn't fill me with dread. Instead, it felt like a step forward—a way to honor her memory without being consumed by it.

The drive back was quieter than usual, the team lost in their thoughts as the miles rolled by. When we finally reached home, the weight of the investigation lifted, replaced by the comfort of familiar surroundings. The van was unloaded, the equipment stored, and we all parted ways with promises to catch up soon.

That evening, I sat in my living room with Gabby perched on the back of the couch. A cup of tea steamed in my hands, and for the first time in what felt like forever, I allowed myself to just breathe.

"You did good," Gabby said, her tone unusually soft.

"Thanks," I murmured. "We all did."

As the sun set and the room filled with golden light, I felt a sense of peace settle over me. The past wasn't something I could change, but it didn't have to define me either. Sophie would always be a part of me, but so would the team, the work we'd done, and the lives we'd touched.

And as for the future? It didn't feel so heavy anymore. For the first time, it felt wide open, full of possibilities.

Gabby let out a soft coo, and I smiled, the sound a comforting reminder I wasn't alone. Together, we'd faced the darkness—and come out stronger on the other side.

Everything really was okay.

I'd love to stay in touch! **Click here to join my monthly newsletter for updates, sneak peeks, and specials!**

This isn't the end for our Haunted Histories crew, but they are taking a much deserved break! Check out my other paranormal mysteries on the next page.

If you enjoyed this book, please consider leaving a review or star rating. It's one of the best ways to support independent authors and it lets others know if they might also enjoy this book.

*Scan the QR code above to discover more books by
Lynn M. Stout.*

*Scan above to receive sneak peeks, updates, and
special deals by joining my monthly newsletter!*

Find more books by Lynn M. Stout and other cozy
mystery authors at the independent book store
dedicated to cozy mystery readers! **Visit Mystic**
Valley Press by scanning the code above.